Over in the Meadow

A Traditional Counting Rhyme

Adapted and Illustrated by
Jan Thornhill

Owl
kids

Owlkids Books Inc.
10 Lower Spadina Avenue, Suite 400, Toronto, Ontario M5V 2Z2
www.owlkidsbooks.com

Distributed in Canada by University of Toronto Press
5201 Dufferin Street, Toronto, Ontario M3H 5T8

Distributed in the United States by Publishers Group West
1700 Fourth Street, Berkeley, California 94710

Over in the Meadow is a traditional southern Appalachian counting rhyme popularized
at the turn of the last century by Olive A. Wadsworth.

Library and Archives Canada Cataloguing in Publication

Thornhill, Jan
     Over in the meadow : a traditional counting rhyme / adapted
& illustrated by Jan Thornhill.

Based on the rhyme by Olive A. Wadsworth.
Issued also in electronic format.
ISBN 978-1-926973-06-7

     1. Counting-out rhymes. 2. Animals--Juvenile poetry. I. Wadsworth,
Olive A., 1835-1886. Over in the meadow. II. Title.

PS8589.H5497O93 2012   jC811'.54   C2011-904931-7

Illustration, original type, and book design: Jan Thornhill

Canadian Heritage / Patrimoine canadien

Canada Council for the Arts / Conseil des Arts du Canada

Canadä

ONTARIO ARTS COUNCIL
CONSEIL DES ARTS DE L'ONTARIO

Ontario
Ontario Media Development Corporation
Société de développement de l'industrie des médias de l'Ontario

We acknowledge the financial support of the Canada Council for the Arts, the Ontario Arts Council, the Government
of Canada through the Canada Book Fund (CBF) and the Government of Ontario through the Ontario Media
Development Corporation's Book Initiative for our publishing activities.

Manufactured by WKT Co. Ltd.
Manufactured in Shenzhen, Guangdong, China, in July 2012
Job #12CB0972

B   C   D   E   F

Publisher of Chirp, chickaDEE and OWL
www.owlkidsbooks.com

For more than a hundred years, *Over in the Meadow* has been a joyous introduction for young children to counting, to rhyming, and to animal babies. In this version, I've tried to add another dimension by building each of the illustrations out of common, everyday objects. A baby crow is created from prunes and carrots, with a button for an eye. A fly's head is a radio; its body, a pine cone.

I hope children will find as much enjoyment in visually taking apart these illustrations as I had in making them. And, oh, by the way, after being photographed, everything edible in the book was eaten!

Jan Thornhill

Over in the meadow
the sun came up.

Over in the meadow
in the sand in the sun,
lived an old mother
turtle and her
little turtle one.
"Dig!" said the mother.
"We dig!" said the 1.
So they dug all day in the
sand in the sun.

Over in the meadow
where the stream runs blue,
lived an old mother fish
and her little fishies two.
"Swim!" said the mother.
"We swim!" said the 2.
So they swam all day where
the stream runs blue.

Over in the meadow
in a hole in a tree,
lived an old mother Owl
and her little owls three.
"Hoo-hoo!" said the mother.
"We hoo-hoo!" said the 3.
So they hoo-hooed all day
in the hole in the tree.

Over in the meadow
by an old barn door,
lived an old mother mouse
and her little mice four.
"Gnaw!" said the mother.
"We gnaw!" said the 4.
So they gnawed all day
by the old barn door.

Over in the meadow
by a box beehive,
lived an old mother 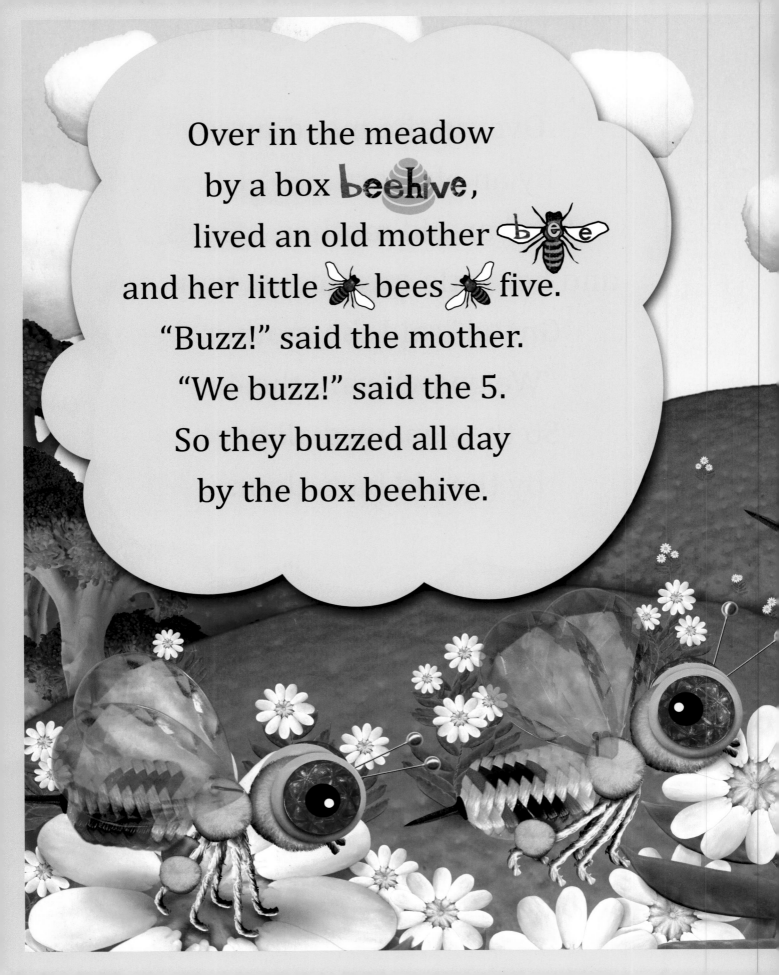 bee
and her little bees five.
"Buzz!" said the mother.
"We buzz!" said the 5.
So they buzzed all day
by the box beehive.

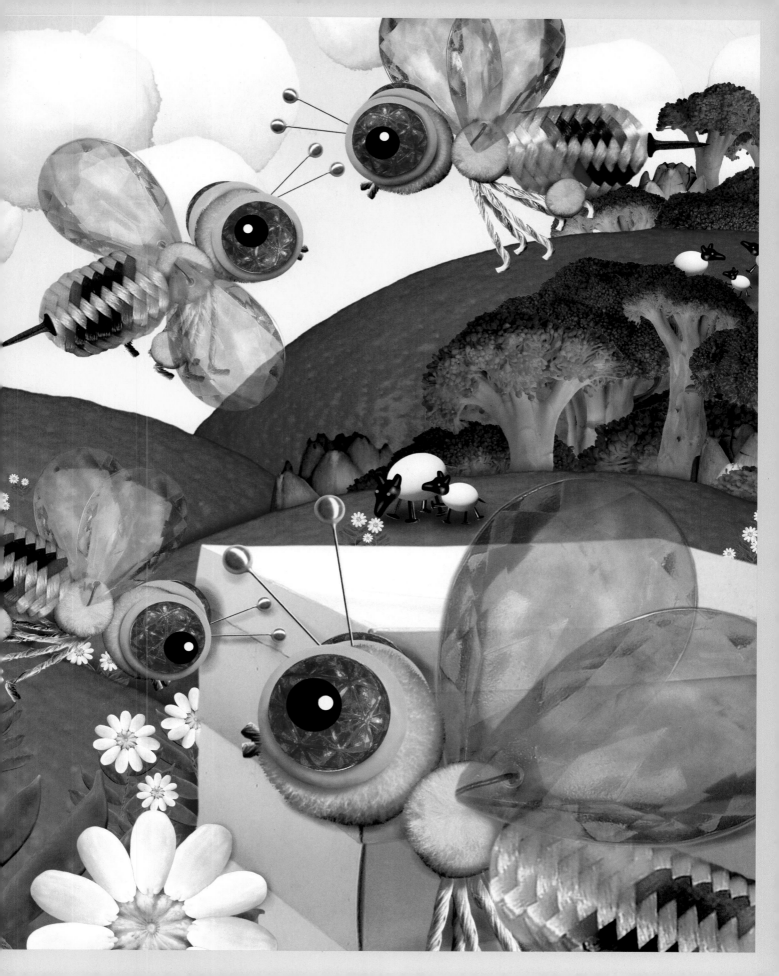

Over in the meadow
in a nest built of sticks,
lived an old mother crow
and her little crows six.
"Caw!" said the mother.
"We caw!" said the 6.
So they cawed all day in the
nest built of sticks.

Over in the meadow
where the grass grows so even,
lived an old mother frog
and her little froggies seven.
"Jump!" said the mother.
"We jump!" said the 7.
So they jumped all day where
the grass grows so even.

Over in the meadow
by the old mossy gate,
lived an old mother  lizard
and her little lizards eight.
"Bask!" said the mother.
"We bask!" said the 8.
So they basked all day
by the old mossy gate.

Over in the meadow
by an old Scotch pine,
lived an old mother duck
and her little duckies nine.
"Quack!" said the mother.
"We quack!" said the 9.
So they quacked all day
by the old Scotch pine.

Over in the meadow
by a cozy wee den,
lived an old mother beaver
and her little beavers ten.
"Chew!" said the mother.
"We chew!" said the 10.
So they chewed all day
by their cozy wee den.

Over in the meadow
the sun went down.

Where is it?

All of the pictures in this book were created on a computer using photographs of common objects. Many of these objects have been changed. Some have been made bigger or smaller. Some have had their color altered. Some have had parts cut off. Can you find where the objects on these pages were used?

cheese snacks

pretzels

dustpan & brush

fried egg

bow

seeds & grains

magazine eyes

berries

marbles

beads

glass-headed pins

carpet tacks

comb

cutlery

twist ties

teacup

avocado

snow peas

banana

garlic

green beans

pine cones

squash

artichoke

lime

broccoli

rope

thread

twine

radio

seashells

nail clippers

paper clips

scissors

candy

popsicle

paper

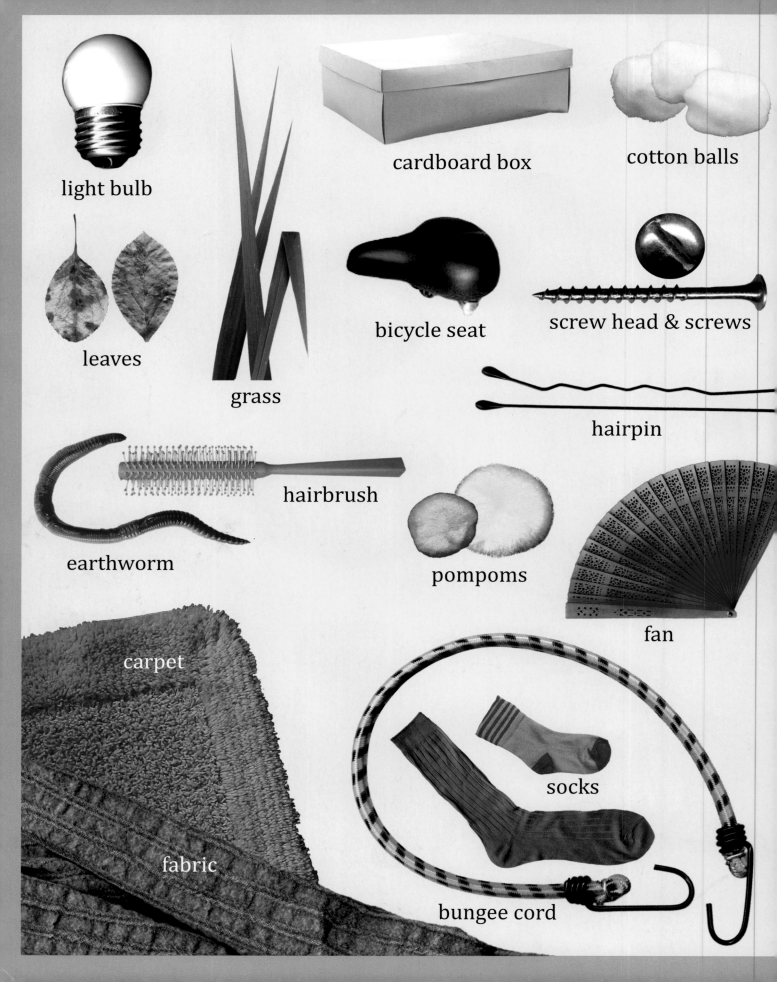

light bulb

cardboard box

cotton balls

leaves

grass

bicycle seat

screw head & screws

hairpin

earthworm

hairbrush

pompoms

fan

carpet

fabric

socks

bungee cord

necktie

hair-ties

chili peppers

rubber bands

toothpicks

coffee

more leaves

slippers

reflector

nuts

brown sugar

shoelaces

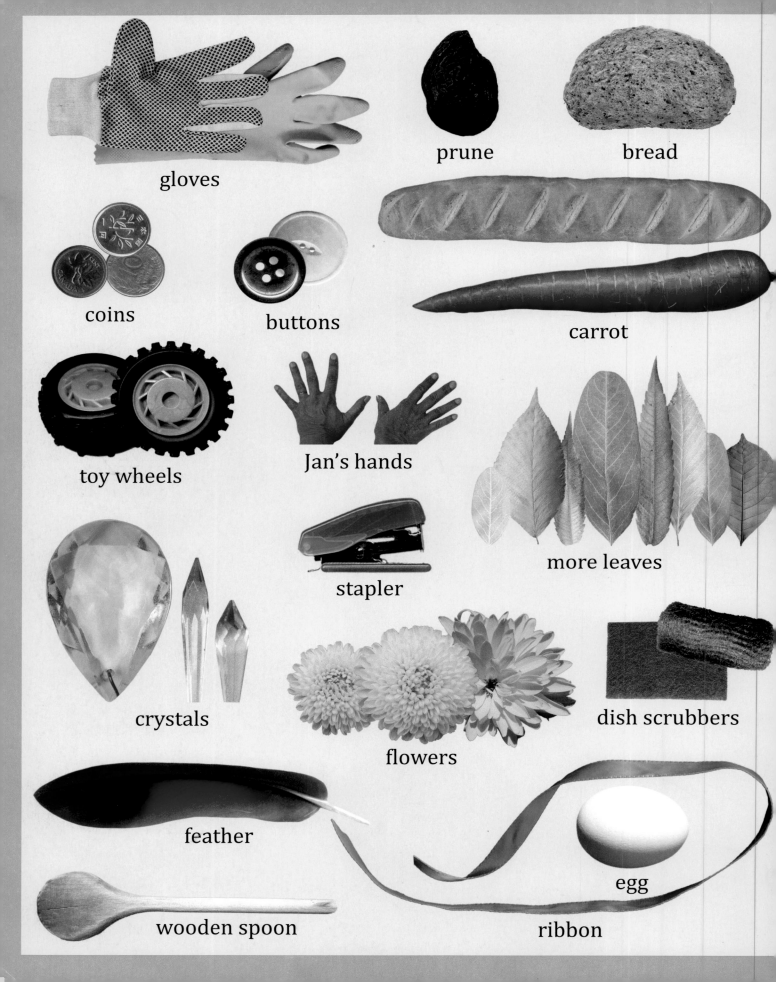

gloves

prune

bread

coins

buttons

carrot

toy wheels

Jan's hands

more leaves

crystals

stapler

flowers

dish scrubbers

feather

egg

wooden spoon

ribbon